the EIGHTH MENORAH

Lauren L. Wohl   illustrated by *Laura Hughes*

ALBERT WHITMAN & COMPANY
CHICAGO, ILLINOIS

For Cliff, and for the Hanukkahs past and all those to come. —LLW

For Nana and Grandma. —LH

Library of Congress Cataloging-in-Publication Data

Wohl, Lauren L.
The eighth menorah / by Lauren L. Wohl ; illustrated by Laura Hughes.
pages cm
Summary: Sam is reluctant to make a menorah in Sunday School
because his family already owns seven, but after a conversation with his
grandmother, he figures out how to make a perfect Hanukkah gift.
[1. Menorah—Fiction. 2. Hanukkah—Fiction. 3. Jews—United States—Fiction.]
I. Hughes, Laura, illustrator. II. Title.
PZ7.W8176Eig 2013
[E]—dc23
2013005188

Text copyright 2013 by Lauren L. Wohl.
Illustrations copyright 2013 by Albert Whitman & Company.
Published in 2013 by Albert Whitman & Company.
ISBN 978-0-8075-1892-2

Printed in China.
10 9 8 7 6 5 4 3 2 1 HH 18 17 16 15 14 13

For more information about Albert Whitman & Company,
visit our web site at www.albertwhitman.com.

One November day at Hebrew school, Sam's class had a treasure hunt in the park.

Everyone found pebbles of different shapes and sizes, pinecones, acorns, and twigs. Sam found a small, shiny sliver of rock that danced with silver specks.

Back in the classroom on the second floor of the temple, they rinsed their treasures in the sink and set them out to dry on paper towels.

The twigs and pinecones turned a deep, rich brown. The acorns sparkled in the light. The pebbles shimmered. Sam's rock glowed. "Next week, we're going to decorate our own Hanukkah menorahs with all these treasures," Sam's teacher, Ms. Zuckerman, explained. "They will make wonderful surprises for your parents."

Menorahs? Sam's family already had lots of menorahs. They didn't need another one.

The next Sunday, Ms. Zuckerman showed the children a brick of clay decorated with buttons and marbles and little jewels. On the top, they counted one, two, three, four, five, six, seven, eight, nine holes.

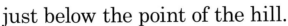

"I made this menorah when I was in Sunday school," Ms. Z. said. "Now it's your turn to make one."

Sam raised his hand. "My family has a menorah. My family has seven menorahs! Maybe I can make something else."

"Don't worry, Sam," Ms. Z. told him. "You'll see. Your parents will love it."

Sam wasn't so sure.

The children began shaping their blocks of clay into menorahs. Sam watched Rebecca turn hers into a snake and Danny turn his into a circle. Sam used a wooden tool to create a hill out of his clay. He placed his silvery rock just below the point of the hill.

That afternoon, Sam's grandmother called.
Sam told her, "Grammy, I have a secret."
"I love secrets, Sammy," Grammy said.
"It's about what we're making in Hebrew
school," Sam added.
"May I guess?"
"Sure."
"Is it a painting?"
"Nope."

"Is it a puppet?"

"Nuh uh."

"Is it something to eat?
I think it's something to eat."

"No."

"I give up, Sam. What is it?"

"It's a secret, Grammy."

When the children came in the next week, the menorahs were lined up on Ms. Zuckerman's desk. They looked like a celebration about to happen.

"All that's left to do is wrap them," Ms. Z. said.

"But, Ms. Z., my family already has seven menorahs. All of them are special."

"Don't fret, Sam. Look at it! Imagine how it will shine with the candles lit."

It was a pretty great menorah, Sam had to admit.

"Now comes the hardest part," Ms. Zuckerman reminded them. "Hanukkah is not for three weeks. When you take your menorah home, you need to find a hiding place for it."

Sam knew just the right place to hide his menorah.

"Hi, Grammy. How are you doing? Did you make any new friends in your building?"

"I did! I went shopping with a couple of my new neighbors today. I'm going to bake you a surprise."

"What?"

"You'll see. And talking about surprises, how's your secret coming along?" Grammy asked.

"It's done. I've got it here in a hiding place waiting for Hanukkah."

"Oh," Grammy said. "A Hanukkah present."

"For Mom and Dad," Sam said. Then he added, "Don't tell."

"Never," Grammy promised.

The next Sunday Ms. Zuckerman announced, "Time to get ready for Hanukkah."

She told the class the story of the brave Maccabees and their fight to save the Temple.

She told them about the miracle of the oil; how the little bit of it that should have lasted only one day in the eternal lamp lasted for eight days.

She taught them the songs "Rock of Ages" and "I Have a Little Dreidel."

They practiced the prayers for the candle lighting.

"What's new, Sammy?" Grammy asked when she called that week.

"We're having a Hanukkah party on Sunday."

"Sounds like fun. I love Hanukkah. But I'm afraid this year the holiday will be very different. The condo I moved into doesn't allow open flames in our apartments. I won't be able to light candles."

"How come?" Sam wondered.

"Safety rules. But there is an electric menorah in the community room."

"No candles allowed there either, Grammy?"

"Yes. You can have candles there. But they tell me everyone just uses the electric menorah."

"Oh. You can light candles at our house. You're coming over for the first night, right?"

"I am. And that will be very nice. Thank you, Sammy."

On the Sunday of their party, Ms. Zuckerman brought in potato latkes. All the children had a feast.

The children played dreidel for Hanukkah gelt. Sam won five pieces of chocolate.

As everyone was leaving, Ms. Z. handed each child a box of Hanukkah candles. She winked at the children and told them quietly, "Don't forget the secret presents."

Sam's stomach dropped.

Sam checked under his bed when he got home. His menorah was there—safe and sound.

"Sam, we need your help, please," his dad called.

All the family's menorahs were lined up on the dining room table. "Which one do you think we should use this year, Sam?" his dad asked.

One had been his mom's when she was a girl. One came from Russia with his great-great-grandmother. His grammy and grandpa brought one home from their trip to Israel.

The one with the animals had been his dad's when he was a boy. One was the menorah his parents bought for their first Hanukkah together. And one was a gift from Nana and Poppy.

The smallest one was the menorah Sam's parents had bought when Sam was born.

Sam was now more certain than ever that his parents didn't need a menorah with twigs and pebbles and one silvery rock.

But he *did* know someone who could use it.

On the first evening of the holiday,
Sam and his parents drove to Grammy's condo
to pick her up. She was waiting for them in the lobby.
"Can we go to the community room to see the electric
menorah, Grammy?"

Grammy took Sam's hand and they walked
toward a big double door.

Sam reached into the bag he was carrying and handed her a package. "This is for you, Grammy," he said.

"Oh, Sammy. Thank you!"

Grammy opened the package slowly and carefully.

"A menorah," she said. She held it up and looked
at it for a long while, and then she said. "It is just
beautiful!"

"I made it," Sam said proudly.

"In Hebrew school?" Grammy asked, smiling.

"It's the secret, Grammy."

"It's the best secret ever."

Grammy hugged Sam.

Sammy noticed that some of Grammy's neighbors were coming in to the community room. They admired the menorah.

"Can we light it now?" he asked everyone.

"We can," Grammy said. "But we don't have candles."

Sam reached into his bag again and took out the box of candles Ms. Zuckerman had given him.

They set up the menorah and put the shamash candle at the top of the hill, just above Sam's shiny rock. They put one more candle in the first hole.

Then Sam, his mom, dad, and grandma, along with Grammy's new friends, lit the candles and sang the blessings together.

Mr. Levine, one of Grammy's neighbors, shook Sam's hand. "This is the best Hanukkah gift ever, Sam. I hope you don't mind if we all share it." He bent down and kissed Sam on the top of his head.

Sam heard him whisper to his grammy, "You've got quite a mensch there."

Sam looked at his lighted menorah. The silvery rock sparkled. Everyone's eyes brightened too.

HOW TO PLAY DREIDEL

   One of Hanukkah's traditions is to play games of dreidel. A dreidel is a four-sided top with a different Hebrew letter on each side. They are:

נ: Nun

ג: Gimel

ה: Hay

ש: Shin

The letters stand for words which make up a sentence:
   NES GADOL HAYA SHAM

This means:
   "A great miracle happened there."

The letters also stand for actions in the game of dreidel:

נ Nun means do nothing

ג Gimel means take the whole pot

ה Hay means take half the pot

ש Shin means add a coin to the pot

   Each player begins with five pieces of Hanukkah gelt—chocolate covered in foil to look like coins. Each player puts one piece of gelt into the center, or the pot. The first player spins the dreidel. When it stops, the player takes the action of the letter that is showing. If it's נ (nun), she does nothing. If it's ה (hay), she takes half the coins in the pot, and so on.
   Each player takes a turn. When the pot is empty, each player adds a coin. When one person has won everything, the game is over.

A happy game of dreidel, come play now, let's begin!